Adventure in

LEGOLAND®

**Other books in the
Shooting Star series:**

Adventure in

LEGOLAND®

by Carol Matas
illustrated by Mark Teague

Scholastic Canada Ltd.

Canadian Cataloguing in Publication Data

Matas, Carol, 1949-
  Adventure in Legoland

ISBN 0-590-74260-4

I. Teague, Mark II. Title.

PS8576.A73A68 1992   jC813'.54   C91-095501-8
PZ7.M3Ad 1992

9 8 7 6 5 4 3 2 1   Printed in USA   2 3 4 5 6 7/9

For my son (Aaron) Sam Brask
And for his best friend,
Aryeh Kobrinsky

The author wishes to acknowledge the
Manitoba Arts Council
for their financial assistance,
and Preben Dewald Hansen of LEGO Publishing
for his invaluable help and generosity.

Contents

1

A CRY FOR HELP

"Help. Help."

Aaron sat up in bed.

"Help."

The room was dark, his father was snoring, his mother and sister were sound asleep.

"Please *help.*"

It was a tiny voice, thin and sweet. Who was in trouble? He tiptoed over to his sister's bed.

"Rebecca. Rebecca. Wake up. Wake up."

She didn't stir. He shook her. "Wake up." Still she didn't move.

He went over and shook his mother by the shoulder.

"Mom. Mom." Then his dad. Nothing. What was the matter with them? His mother usually woke up if he tiptoed past her room at night to go to the bathroom. Why wouldn't she wake up now?

They were all in the same room because they were staying overnight at a hotel in Legoland. Aaron's family had come from Winnipeg, Canada, to Denmark to visit Aaron's grandparents. They had driven up to Legoland that day, from Copenhagen.

Maybe they're all too tired to wake up, Aaron thought. It had been a long drive. Once they'd arrived, they'd gone to eat at the restaurant, and Aaron had gotten into lots of trouble because he wouldn't sit still. The people at the next table had called Aaron wild. Well, he was used to that.

"Help. Help."

Someone needed help. Perhaps he should check the hallway. He tried once more to wake his mother. He shook her arm up and down. It really was strange that he couldn't wake her. Could they all be *that* tired?

They had had a very exciting day. After dinner they had gone to the Legoland Park, an amusement park. Aaron could never have imagined anything like it, and Aaron had a very good imagination.

The Legoland Park had many different areas. Everything was made out of Lego blocks. There was a Safari Park filled with almost life-sized elephants, giraffes, lions, and other animals. Miniland was made up of castles and entire towns from different places in Europe, all in minia-ture, just the right size for Lego people.

Fabuland had rides for young children. Legoredo was a western town with real old-fashioned buildings, pony rides, and a mine where you could search for gold.

Aaron and Rebecca went on as many rides as they could before the park closed at eight P.M. Afterwards they were able to get a quick look at some of the indoor displays. The one that really caught Aaron's eye was Titania's Palace.

It was a huge dollhouse, built up on a stand so people could look in without bending over. There was a bar running around it to keep people from touching it, and a footrest for little kids to stand on as they peered inside.

Each room was done in perfect detail — playrooms for the children, a dining room, a library, a den, a throne room, bedrooms, bathrooms, even an indoor garden with a kangaroo — but all in miniature so that most of the objects were no bigger than Aaron's fingernail.

"Help."

Perhaps a child was lost. Aaron groped around the floor looking for his sneakers. He found them and put them on. He thought of changing out of his pajamas but knew he'd never find any clothes in the dark. Besides, he wasn't ashamed to be seen in his Superman pajamas. He liked them better than most of his clothes.

Gently Aaron turned the lock and opened the door. He peeked out into the long hallway. No one was there, but the voice was clearer, more urgent.

"Help. Please."

The room was in the middle of the hall. Aaron hesitated as he stepped out. He saw nothing. The voice seemed to be coming from behind the door at the end of the hall, which led to the hotel lobby. He hurried toward it, pulled the big door, and

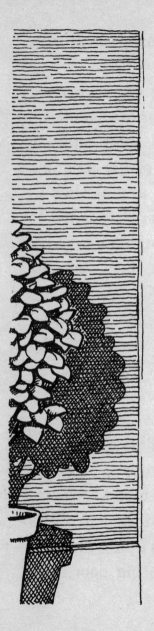

entered the lobby. All was quiet and empty.

The reception desk was around the corner. The voice seemed to be coming from straight ahead and to his left. Aaron moved past the brown couches, the empty dining room, down the hallway toward the overpass to the Legoland Park.

The voice was louder now. His heart was pounding and he shivered a little even though it was warm in the hotel. He walked up to the glass door that led to the stairs. It was open just a crack. Shouldn't it be locked, he thought? He pushed it open, walked slowly up the red carpeted stairs and into the passageway filled with exhibits.

The passageway was fully lit. As he walked past the Lego soldiers, the Lego pandas, the Lego penguins, the Lego Viking; they all seemed so lifelike he thought perhaps they would begin to

7

move. Even the clowns looked spooky to him. He almost expected them to reach out and grab him.

Aaron hurried through the passageway, walked under the huge Lego map of Denmark, and cautiously moved down the stairs. He could still hear the voice, even more clearly than before. He paused at the bottom of the stairs.

Legoland Park stood before him, quiet and eerie in the moonlight. The glass doors were closed now, and the sound was definitely coming from his right.

The room he was standing in was full of glass cases containing exhibits. He walked past them, into a room filled with old-fashioned toys enclosed in glass bubbles. It was dark except for the exit signs, and he kept bumping into the display cases. He felt more and more jumpy by the minute. Everything was so quiet and empty, except for that voice. It sounded louder and louder every second. Finally he reached the room that housed Titania's Palace.

"Help. Help."

It sounded as if the voice were coming straight from the dollhouse palace itself. To his surprise, the palace was all lit up from within. He tiptoed forward. He stared, rubbed his eyes, and stared again.

There was movement in the palace. There was a hustle and bustle. Then the voice suddenly stopped. Aaron stepped up onto the footrest for a better view, and looked into the garden.

Two small children, a boy and a girl, were playing catch with a small gold ball. The boy looked around five, the girl a little younger. She kept dropping the ball or losing it in the shrubbery. The girl was dressed in a pale pink silk dress with pink stockings. The boy wore blue satin riding pants, a blue satin vest, and a white silk

blouse with puffy sleeves. They both wore little gold slippers on their feet.

The strangest thing about them apart from their size, which couldn't have been more than two inches tall, was that they each had a pair of translucent wings attached to their backs.

"Help."

The voice came loud and clear once more, and jolted Aaron out of his shock. He stood, staring at the tiny children for a long time, not believing what he saw.

It sounded as if the voice came from a room in the palace, just around the corner. He moved towards it, half terrified, half thrilled. Was it possible? Was what he was seeing real? Perhaps he was dreaming. He stopped and thought about that. Yes, perhaps he was dreaming and he'd soon wake up.

"You aren't dreaming," a sweet voice said in his ear.

2

THE FAIRY QUEEN

"What?!" Aaron screamed, jumping away from the voice that had spoken in his ear.

"Don't be afraid." A fairy was hovering in front of him. "My name is Martha. I'm Queen Titania's maid. I'm to bring you to our Queen."

"Me?" Aaron gulped. What could a queen want with me? he thought.

The fairy had a little cup in her hand. "Will you drink this?" she asked.

"Why?" Aaron answered, immediately

suspicious. He hated medicine; he also hated many foods and had been told *never* to take food or candy from a stranger. Surely there couldn't be anything stranger than this fairy.

"It will shrink you," the maid explained. Aaron noticed she was wearing a white apron, which covered her long black dress.

"Shrink me?" he exclaimed. "I don't want to shrink. I'm trying to grow!"

"It only works for twelve hours. The effect will wear off then, and you'll be back to normal. Of course, Her Majesty would be delighted to invite you in as you are, but it's quite impossible. You'd never fit."

Aaron knew that was true. But did he want to shrink? And why should he?

"But why?" he asked the maid.

"Her Majesty must explain it all to you. She needs help and has been calling for hours. You are the only one who answered the call."

"Why?" Aaron repeated. It was just about his favorite word.

"I don't know," replied the maid, beginning to get annoyed. "I suppose you're the only one who heard it. Although how a little boy like you can help is beyond me. You're too young to be of any use at all."

When Aaron heard that, he grabbed the tiny cup and drank down its contents. No one was going to tell *him* he was too young! That was all he heard every day from his sister. It drove him crazy. Well, he'd show them. If someone needed help, he would help. He felt a drop or two of liquid slide down his throat.

"Oh," he said, "that's not enough to do anything!"

But all of a sudden he had a terrible feeling of everything scrunching up, and of the whole world getting very big. Then he was scooped up in the maid's arms and flown into the palace. He was put down in a small room, which he recognized as Titania's sitting room.

A young woman sat in the white armchair, staring into the fire. Absently she stroked the King Charles spaniel that sat on her lap. Aaron looked at it in surprise. At home, his friend Dov had three dogs just like it. He'd told Aaron the King Charles spaniel was the dog of royalty.

The woman's face was pale, her mouth drawn in a thin line of worry, but still Aaron thought she was very beautiful. Her hair, a deep chestnut brown, cascaded in waves down her back. She shook her head, as if she were talking to herself.

"Ahem," the maid said.

The woman lifted her sea-green eyes, and looked at her maid. She straightened up when she noticed Aaron.

"And who is this?"

"This is a boy who heard the call, Your Highness."

Your Highness! Aaron couldn't believe it. He was in the presence of the Queen. What should he do? Bow? Yes, everyone bowed when they saw a queen. Awkwardly he bent over, then straightened.

"No, no ceremony is necessary," the Queen said, her voice soft. "Please come closer."

There was a little footstool by her chair, and two tables on either side, so Aaron didn't find it easy to get very close. He moved around them and stood with his back to the fire, feeling its heat.

"What's your name, my dear?" the Queen said gently.

"Aaron. Aaron Samuel."

"Well, Aaron, have you come to help?"

"Well, yes," Aaron answered bravely.

"And what kind of boy are you?" she asked.

"The wild kind," he answered, with great certainty.

"The wild kind?" she repeated, and almost looked like she would laugh, except she was too worried to do so. "What makes you say that?"

"Well, everyone says so," Aaron replied. "My teachers especially. I'm wild. I can't sit still, I bug my sister, and I yell too much. I run too much. I scream too much. I won't go to sleep at night. My teachers say I ask too many questions."

"Stop. Stop." Queen Titania laughed.

Then she looked at him seriously. "But you were the one who heard our call. So you are special. Maybe," she said and smiled, "it's because you are so wild."

Aaron wasn't sure whether she was joking or not. He was always so different from all his friends. They were quiet, well behaved, and rarely got into trouble. He always did. And now it was the same. Out of everyone in the entire hotel, he was the only one who had heard the call — why? Why did he always have to be different?

"Sometimes," said Queen Titania, "being different is a very good thing."

Aaron started. Had she read his mind? The maid had done the same thing.

"I have a son," said Queen Titania, "just your age." She paused and he thought he saw a tear form in her eye. "He's been kidnapped by Bad Bart from Legoredo. Will you go and rescue him?"

3

WILL YOU GO?

"You want me to rescue your son?" Aaron echoed the Queen, hardly believing his ears. "From Bad Bart?" He stopped to think for a moment. "How bad *is* Bad Bart?"

"*Very* bad," Queen Titania replied. "Only a *very* bad person would kidnap a little child. You see, my husband Oberon is away in Copenhagen visiting relatives in Tivoli. But he couldn't go after our son Aryeh, anyway."

"Why not?" Aaron wondered aloud. He

also wondered why the Queen couldn't go. She seemed to have a lot of servants who would watch her other children while she was away.

"You see, Bad Bart has invented a kind of fairy poison. He told us this in his ransom note. Would you like to hear it?"

"Yes, please," said Aaron.

The maid ran over to one of the desks in the room and quickly brought the note to the Queen. The Queen read:

Madame —

I have taken your son. Do not try to follow us, he will soon be beyond your reach. I have invented a fairy poison. It is a spray. It will first crumple your wings, next your muscles, next your bones. It is deadly to you. I want you to send me all your jewelry, all your gold and silver. Then I promise to return your son.

Yours truly,
Bad Bart

"Bad guys never keep their promises," Aaron said.

"Yes," Queen Titania agreed, "you're so right. And you know, if I give him everything, think how disappointed all the people would be who come here in the day to look at my beautiful palace. I would do it though," she added, "if I thought he would keep his promise. But perhaps he will keep Aryeh and just continue asking for more and more things.

"And perhaps," she continued very sadly, "he will try to make Aryeh enjoy shooting and robbing and even get him to join his gang. So you see, rescuing my Aryeh is the only answer. *We* cannot do it. And if we ask the Lego people for help, Bad Bart is sure to hear about it. We need someone from outside who will work alone."

"All alone?" Aaron sputtered. How could he admit to the Queen that he was afraid of the dark — and had always been scared of being kidnapped himself? What if he should get kidnapped, too?

"Here is something that will help you," said the Queen, going to her writing table. She quickly wrote a little note and then stamped it. She handed it to Aaron. He saw that it was written on her own personal stationery that had the royal seal. It read, "To whom it may concern: The bearer of this letter is entitled to any help he may ask for. Also, if payment is needed for any service rendered please come to the palace and the Royal Treasurer will pay you. Signed, Queen Titania."

"Here you are," she said. Aaron folded the note and carefully put it in his pocket.

"Now, as for your dress, it is a warm night but I do think you could use a jacket. Martha, please fetch one of Aryeh's."

Martha hurried off. Aaron stood and stared at the Queen. He knew she would now ask him the question.

"Will you go?" she said.

For a moment he couldn't speak. He was certainly scared. He was only eight. He hated the dark. He hated bad guys . . . how could he ever do it?

"You are the only one that answered the call," the Queen reminded him. "There must be a reason for that. I'm sure you have the best chance."

Aaron was so used to people saying "Don't do this, don't do that!" that when the Queen said she was sure he *could* do it, somehow, he heard himself agree.

"All right," he said, his voice small and unsure. "I'll try."

"Good." She smiled. "Now then, don't worry. It won't be a dark or terrible journey. Legoland comes alive at night for Lego people. I'm sure you'll find the boats working, the trains going. It won't be too hard to get to Legoredo. Once you are there, find the sheriff. He's a good man and he'll do all he can to rescue my boy."

Just then Martha hurried in with a thick blue suede jacket. Aaron put it on.

"Martha will show you the way into Legoland," the Queen said. She offered Aaron her hand and he shook it.

"Good-bye, Aaron. Good luck."

"Good-bye, Your Majesty," Aaron replied. With great dignity, he turned to follow Martha.

Aaron didn't feel dignified for long because he tripped over the carpet and fell flat on his face.

Great start, he thought to himself. He scrambled up, and without looking back ran after Martha. She didn't seem to be heading for the door. Instead she walked straight to the wall, pressed a panel, and a secret door opened. She walked through, and Aaron followed.

He found himself in a chapel all lit up with candles. The walls were painted in reds and golds. There seemed to be gold everywhere. There was even a large gold organ.

"I'm taking you this way so that we see as few people as possible," Martha whispered. "We don't want Bad Bart to hear that you're on your way to the sheriff."

"No, we don't," Aaron agreed.

Martha then picked Aaron up, and they flew back through the room full of old-fashioned toys. Much to his surprise, he saw that all the toys were alive. The carriages were moving, the clowns were juggling, the bands were playing, the trains were chugging. He would have been very happy if Martha had just put him down there to watch everything. But she carried him into the next room. The glass doors leading to Legoland were open and all the buildings were now lit.

Martha set Aaron down. That's when he realized how small he really was.

"I'll never get there," he groaned. "I'm too little. It'll take me all night."

"You wouldn't be allowed in Legoland now if you were big," Martha said, "because you could squash people by accident."

"Are all the people the same size as you?" Aaron asked. He remembered the monorail he'd been on that day. Almost all the rides were big — made for children or even adults.

"All the night people are about our size," Martha replied. "Most people, outside of the fairies, live in Miniland, because everything is just the right size for them. Some found it too dull there so they left and went to Legoredo. Everything there is built for big people, but somehow they manage. It used to be a place where people worked hard, but enjoyed themselves, too. Then Bad Bart showed up. He's small like the rest, but mean and nasty in his heart."

"Where did he show up from?" Aaron asked.

"No one knows," Martha answered. "Look, I shouldn't do this, but I think it'll take you too long to walk all the way. I'll fly you to Miniland and you can find your way from there, all right?"

"I wouldn't want your wings to get poisoned," Aaron said.

"I'll take a chance," Martha answered, "because I love Aryeh and I want him back. Let's hope Bad Bart doesn't have spies this close to the palace." She picked up Aaron again and flew over the large grass, over the walkways, over the large railroad tracks, and set him down in Miniland next to the Nyhavn Canal. Once there Aaron no longer felt small. He knew he was, but the buildings looked exactly as they did in Copenhagen, except they were made just for his tiny size. He felt much better.

"Good-bye, Aaron," Martha said. "And good luck."

Aaron watched her fly away. Now he was really on his own. He had to get to Legoredo as fast as he could. He had to find the sheriff. What was the quickest way there? Where should he go first?

4

THE AIRPORT

Aaron looked around him. He was standing at the top of the street of Nyhavn Harbor. It was so busy that no one had noticed his arrival.

On the other hand, Aaron couldn't help but stare at the Lego people who were alive and walking around. They moved stiffly because their knees and arms didn't bend. He saw one man leaning over to pick up something. The man had to bend straight over from the waist. Then he saw a little boy, searching for his dog.

The boy's head twirled all around in a full circle as he called his dog's name.

"Rufus, here boy, here boy."

Aaron noticed that when the boy opened his mouth, he even had teeth. In fact the two front ones were missing.

Mostly the people's faces were yellow and had little black dots for eyes and little black smiles. All their legs had holes in the back. Aaron knew that was so they could snap onto other Lego pieces.

Boats were docking or setting off. People sat and visited on the benches at the harbor. Tourists climbed into the canal boat. All the shops along the waterfront were open and so were the restaurants. Aaron looked at the tables set so invitingly outside of the cafes. He was hungry.

There was a hot dog stand across the street. Aaron loved the hot dogs in Denmark, especially ones called French hot dogs. A French hot dog was a long bun with a hole through the middle into which the hot dog was placed.

He decided to use the note of credit Queen Titania had given him to get some food, and maybe some information at the same time. He had to think fast, and fortunately he was a very good thinker. He knew that people here would notice he was a stranger. He would have to make up a story about where he was from. He walked up to the man at the hot dog stand.

"One French hot dog please, and a Jolly Cola."

"Yes, right away," the man answered in good English, but with a heavy Danish accent.

Oh, thought Aaron, I'd forgotten all about people speaking Danish. Queen Titania and Martha spoke such perfect English, I'd forgotten that everyone here would probably speak Danish. Fortunately, the hot dog man's English seemed pretty good.

"This is my first time here," Aaron said.

"Where are you from?" the man asked.

Aaron was ready with his answer. "From the palace," he said. After all, he thought, I need some way to explain why I look so much more like the fairies than like the Lego people. He hoped no one would think it strange that he had no wings.

The hot dog man handed Aaron his hot dog and drink. Aaron reached into his pocket, unfolded the letter, and showed it to the man.

The man smiled at Aaron. "A guest of the Queen, are you?" he said. "Well, well. Of course she's not quite as special as *our* Queen," he added, "but I'm sure she's very nice — for a fairy."

Aaron was shocked. "For a fairy?" he repeated. "And what do you mean, *your* Queen?"

"Well, of course we have a Queen here."
The man grinned. "Why else would we
have such a magnificent castle? Or
maybe you haven't seen it yet? Look, here
comes her guard!"

Sure enough, the members of the
Queen's guard were marching toward
them. They looked just like the guard
Aaron had seen in downtown Copenhagen only a few days earlier.

Aaron was very excited about seeing
them. He especially loved their big, tall,
furry hats.

"So the castle is over there?" Aaron
said, pointing after the guard. "What's
that way?" he asked, pointing in the op-
posite direction.

"Well, that's another castle. The Queen
has two!"

"And that way?" Aaron asked. "What's
behind those buildings?" He pointed at
the buildings that the hot dog stand
faced.

"Well, of course, more canals and the rest of the city. I suppose you came by airplane," the man said.

Aaron remembered visiting the airport earlier that evening when he was his regular size. It was only a few steps away from the harbor.

Suddenly he knew how to get to Legoredo. The airport! There had been helicopters there, too. He'd rent a helicopter. He'd never ridden in one and he'd always wanted to. Legoland was a big place. Even if he found his way through Miniland quickly, it would take him *all* night just to walk through it. But flying — *that* was different. Besides, if he had a helicopter, he'd have a better chance of getting away from Bad Bart and his gang.

Aaron stuffed the rest of the hot dog into his mouth, drank down his Jolly Cola, then turned and started walking. Now that he was small, the airport seemed much farther away from the harbor than it had before. Aaron could see it was going to be a long and difficult walk. Suddenly he stopped. He had an idea.

Maybe he could get a taxi. That's how his family always got to the airport at home. He whirled around and raced back to the hot dog stand.

"Excuse me," he said, not noticing that he was interrupting a person ordering a hot dog, "but could you tell me where there is a taxi stand?"

"Just down at the end of the next street over," was the reply.

Aaron quickly found the line of taxis. He ran up to one driver, who was perched on the car hood and asked, "Can you take me to the airport?"

"Yes," said the man, "but have you got any money? Where are your parents?"

"Well," Aaron had to lie, "I'm meeting them there and this is my money." He showed him the Queen's note.

The man nodded. "Get in, then," he said kindly.

Aaron jumped into the backseat. It was about a ten-minute drive, and Aaron was soon in the airport terminal. It was a large terminal, and very busy.

Fortunately the people who worked there could speak many languages, including English.

Aaron walked up to the counter and spoke to the young woman working there. "I need to hire a helicopter," he said.

She laughed. "Well, young man," she said, "I'm sure a lot of children your age would like to go on a helicopter ride but it doesn't work that way." She paused when she saw how disappointed he looked. "Where do you want to go?"

"To Legoredo," he answered.

"You're in luck," she said. "We have a flight going there nightly. In fact, it leaves in one hour."

"But an hour is too long to wait," Aaron exclaimed.

"Now look," the young woman said, "just where are your parents? I think you're too young to be traveling all by yourself." And she gave him a strange look.

She's probably wondering why I don't look like a Lego person, he thought. I'd better do something fast before she asks too many questions. So he did just what he'd seen his mother do when she had a big fight with the people at the airport in Winnipeg, because they were going to seat the family in the smoking section. Aaron couldn't sit there because of his asthma.

"I want to speak to the manager," he declared.

"What!" she laughed. She wasn't taking him seriously.

"I want to speak to the manager," he

shouted. Aaron's voice could be very loud. He was always getting into trouble for it. But it certainly helped him now.

"All right," she said angrily, "you can see the manager. And you can explain this behavior to her as well." She marched off and returned with an older woman who had gray hair, glasses, and a stern expression.

"What is the problem, young man?" the manager said, looking at Aaron's back to see if he had wings.

"I need to get to Legoredo," Aaron replied. "Look." He took out the Queen's note and handed it to the lady.

"Oh, well, this is different." She smiled sweetly. "I see you can pay for whatever you want. I understand you'd like a helicopter."

"Yes, please," Aaron replied.

"Fine. Wait here and I'll see what can be arranged."

Aaron wasn't very good at waiting, so he paced back and forth. After five minutes, the manager returned.

"We've found a pilot and a helicopter," she announced. "Just go through that door." She pointed to a door just beyond the counter. "The pilot will meet you there."

Aaron hurried through the door and into a small room. Sitting behind a desk was a young Lego woman with short black hair, wearing black leather pants and a black leather jacket.

"Hi," she said, "are you my passenger?"

"Are you the pilot?"

"That's me."

"Then I'm your passenger. Can we go right away? I'm sort of in a hurry."

5

THE HELICOPTER TRIP

"Now why," said the pilot in perfect English, "are you in such a hurry?"

"Hey," Aaron said, "you speak English!"

"That's because I'm from the states — the U.S. of A. I was made in a department store. The people from Legoland were doing an exhibit there and when they packed up *their* stuff, they packed *me* with it. I come from Minneapolis, Minnesota."

Aaron had to bite his tongue. He knew

that Minneapolis was close to Winnipeg, and he wanted to tell her that they were almost neighbors. Last year he had driven there with his parents. Instead he said, "Are you homesick?"

She looked down and nodded. "But I have to make the best of it," she declared, getting up in a stiff movement, "because it's so far away I'll never get back. I'll never get home again."

It was such a sad story, Aaron almost started to cry. He was very homesick himself. He missed his friends, Allison and Stephen, his cousin Jessie, his grandmother, and most of all, his little dog, Jake, a poodle. He got tears in his eyes and, for a minute, he forgot all about what he was supposed to do.

"Come on, kid," she said, slapping his back more forcefully than she realized, because her whole arm swung around and her curved hand was hard, and hurt

Aaron. "Don't take it so hard. Hey, what's your name?"

"Aaron Samuel."

"Well, mine's Kim, short for Kimberly, and I think we'd better get a move on."

"Okay," sighed Aaron. "Hey," he said, suddenly getting an idea, "couldn't you get a big person to mail you back? I mean if you gave them the address of the store and everything?"

Kim laughed. "We can't talk to big people, you goof. You know that! They don't even know we're alive!" Then she looked at him sideways. "Hope you don't mind me asking, but you aren't one of us, that's obvious. You don't have fairy wings, either."

"I'm a fairy's cousin," he said quietly, ashamed he had to lie to her. "Listen," he added, "could you give *me* your address in Minneapolis?"

"Now, what on earth for?" Kim asked.

"You never know — maybe I could help."

She didn't want to hurt his feelings so she sat down, wrote out the name of the department store, the address, and the zip code. She folded the paper and gave it to Aaron.

"There's nothing you can do." She shook her head and sighed. "But anyway, here it is. And thanks for the thought."

Aaron tucked the paper in his pocket.

"Okay," Kim said, "let's go."

He followed her down a long corridor, then outside and onto the tarmac. A huge 747 was taxiing for takeoff.

"Where does that go?" he asked.

"I think that one's headed for Fabuland. That's the longest trip we have," Kim answered. "We use the smaller planes for Legoredo and other places."

Aaron's stomach started to jump around as if there were butterflies in it.

They were approaching the helicopter. Kim buckled Aaron in the seat right beside hers, checked all her instruments, buckled herself up, then started the engine. She was given instructions over the radio. Aaron noticed that everything was made to fit the strange shape of the Lego people's hands.

"Number five-oh-oh-two. You are cleared for takeoff. Flight Path two-three-four."

"Roger, tower," Kim answered, and off they went. Aaron felt as if they were in an elevator going up, very fast. They rose high, hovered over the airport for a moment, then traveled straight ahead. They flew past Nyhavn Harbor and saw a huge castle on the right that Kim said was the one the Legoland Queen actually lived in. On the left was another castle — one Kim said was German.

Then they crossed large railroad

tracks, flying over the wooden bridge that arched over the tracks. Finally they were over Legoredo. It looked huge to Aaron. They flew over a mining village, and Aaron saw the gigantic Lego statue of Sitting Bull. He got a glimpse of the water tower and had a very quick look at Mt. Rushmore. They were all made out of Legos.

When they got closer to the ground, Aaron saw a big open fireplace where little Lego people were baking bread. On Aaron's left was the blacksmith's, and on his right the saloon and music hall. Then the merry-go-round came into view, too large for Lego children, so it wasn't in use. Finally, at the end of the street they saw the sheriff's office. Turning to the right was another street where the Legoredo News, the post office, and the pony express were located.

"Where do you want me to set it down?" Kim asked.

"The sheriff's office, please," answered Aaron. "How long would it have taken me to walk?" he added.

"Oh," she said, "an hour and a half at least. Maybe more."

"Well, I'm sure glad you could take me," he said, "because I don't have that much time."

"Hey, Aaron," said Kim, "you want to tell me what this is all about?"

For a minute, Aaron was tempted to tell her. But then he thought he'd better not. The fewer people that knew, the less chance that Bad Bart would find out. Then he had a horrible thought.

"Say," he said as the helicopter touched down in front of the sheriff's office, "is this pretty unusual, a helicopter coming in? Will everyone notice?"

"Yeah, sure, everyone will notice," Kim replied. "After all, it's not the regular flight. That comes in an hour."

Oh boy, Aaron thought, great. Why didn't I think of that? Bad Bart or his pals will see me going into the sheriff's office. They'll get suspicious. Maybe it'll ruin everything.

"Wait!" he yelled. "Take this thing up again. Quick!"

"Okay, okay," Kim exclaimed. "Keep your shirt on!" The helicopter lifted up and hovered over the buildings.

"I don't want to be noticed," Aaron explained.

"Well," Kim answered, "you should have thought of that before. Look."

Aaron followed her gaze and looked down. All the people on the street had stopped to stare at the helicopter. They looked so small surrounded by buildings made for humans. In order to look up, they had to bend all the way backwards from the waist. One or two fell over, hitting their heads on the ground. Fortunately, their heads were plastic and it didn't seem to bother them.

"Oh, great," Aaron groaned, "I'm wrecking everything."

"Look," Kim said, "I think I know what to do. I'm just gonna circle 'round a bit, as though we're sightseeing. Then I'll head out as if we're leaving. There's a forest behind the pony ride, and I'll set the 'copter down there. But you'll have to walk back to the sheriff's office."

"That sounds good," Aaron said thankfully. For a moment, he'd been scared he'd ruined everything. He didn't want Bad Bart knowing about him. Not at all.

Kim did just as she said she would. Aaron wasn't sure he had made the right choice. Flying so low seemed very dangerous. They were flying in between the trees. He began to think that perhaps he should have risked being seen by Bad Bart. Kim did some very fancy flying though, and soon they were on the ground, surrounded by some very large trees. They hadn't seemed so big to Aaron when he was his regular size. But now everything was gigantic.

"How can Lego people live here?" he asked. "It's too big."

"That's why they like it," Kim laughed. "It's different. Some people love a little adventure." She paused. "You gonna be okay?"

"I think so," Aaron replied, trying to make his voice sound more sure than he felt.

"Want me to stay?" she asked. "Or go with you?"

"Oh no, you'd better not go with me," Aaron replied. "I'm supposed to go by myself. But, if you'd wait here . . . well, that would be great."

He was thinking that maybe he'd have another passenger, another boy to fly home.

"Well then, I'll wait," she said.

"Gee," Aaron exclaimed, "that's fantastic! Thanks Kim. I'll see you later — I hope," he added under his breath.

"What?" she said.

"Nothing," he called as he scrambled out of the door she held open for him. "I'll see you later."

The light from the street didn't reach all the way back to the forest, and he had to struggle through tall weeds and high grass, all in semi-darkness. He could see the sheriff's office ahead of him, looming big, gigantic. If he could just get there and find the sheriff. He suddenly had a horrible thought. What if the sheriff wasn't there? What if he couldn't find him? *Then* what would he do?

6

BAD BART

Aaron felt as if he'd never reach the sheriff's office. But after about fifteen minutes he found himself climbing up little Lego steps, which had been placed on the larger big people steps. The door was open. Just inside was a desk, a small jail, and a Lego man with a big cowboy hat, jeans, and a shining star pinned to his leather vest. He leaned back in his chair, chewing on a toothpick, his feet propped up on the desk. Behind him was the big people's desk and the big people's jail.

"Hey, pardner," the man said, smiling. "What can I do for ya? Ya don't live hereabouts — tourist, are ya? Like ma desk? Made it meself!"

"Yes, sir," Aaron replied. "Actually," he said, going right up to the desk and talking very quietly, "I'm not a tourist. I'm here to see *you*. I think. Are you the sheriff?"

"Sure am, son."

"Well," said Aaron, very relieved to have found him, "Queen Titania sent me to see you. Something bad has happened."

The sheriff swung his legs off the desk in one motion, sat up straight, and listened. Of course, when he sat up, his legs stuck straight out ahead of him. It looked so funny to see a person sit that way that for a moment Aaron almost forgot why he was there. A little giggle escaped from his throat.

"And what's that, son?"

"What?" asked Aaron.

"What's happened that's so bad?" the sheriff asked patiently.

"Prince Aryeh has been kidnapped."

"Who by?"

"Bad Bart."

"Why, that's just terrible!" the sheriff exclaimed. "But why did the Queen send you here?"

"Well, I was the only one who answered her call. You see the fairies can't come because Bad Bart has made a poison that will crumple their wings, their muscles, and their bones."

"Oh, he's badder than bad," swore the sheriff. "Well now, I think I know just where Bart's hiding that little fella."

"Where?" asked Aaron.

"His headquarters are at the back of the saloon. He has some rooms, and his men hang 'round there drinking moonshine and keeping lookout so no one can take him by surprise. We'll need to round up a posse of deputies, then go in, and get him." The sheriff straightened his legs so he was standing, and looked all ready to go.

"But couldn't he get hurt that way?" Aaron objected. "There'll be a lot of shooting."

"That's the idea, son. I mean to hurt that varmint."

"No, I mean the Prince," Aaron said.

"Oh, yeah," said the sheriff, "the Prince. Right. Guess maybe we'd better think of another plan."

"How about surprising Bad Bart?" Aaron suggested. "How about sneaking in the back way?"

"Now, that's a right pretty plan," the sheriff nodded. "Yup. I like that. *You* sneak in the back way, grab the boy. Me and my boys'll keep 'em busy out front."

"Me?" Aaron exclaimed. "Well, actually, the Queen said . . . I mean, I was only supposed to tell you — and then you were supposed to — I mean — don't you think one of your deputies should go and get the Prince?"

"Yer right," the sheriff shouted, "of course!" He opened his desk, got out a badge, walked around the desk, and slapped the shining star on Aaron's jacket. Aaron looked. It was stuck on with Velcro.

"There now, you're a deputy. Come on, let's git our horses and ride over to the general store. That's where all my men hang out."

Before Aaron had a chance to object, the sheriff had raced out the door and Aaron had to follow him. They ran down the Lego stairs. Just across the street was a large stable with a mini Lego stable built just beside it. The sheriff grabbed two horses and helped Aaron onto his.

"Ever ridden before, young'un?"

"Well, pony rides — " Aaron started to say.

"Good," the sheriff replied. "She's a great horse. Just follow me."

She was a beautiful horse — white. But hard. A Lego horse. Aaron hung on to the reins as tight as he could. His heart thumped with fear and he hoped his horse wouldn't run away with him. Luckily, she seemed happy to follow the sheriff's brown horse.

They trotted past the merry-go-round. Aaron bounced up and down in the saddle, his behind getting very sore. He had a loose tooth in the back of his mouth, and it occurred to him that this bouncing might cause him to lose it. Everything seemed to be rattling around in his head, even his brains.

The horse soon slowed to a walk, and they arrived at the general store. The sheriff swung himself off his horse, tied both horses to a wooden railing, and told Aaron to wait. The sheriff said he'd be right back.

Well, Aaron had little choice. He didn't see how he could get off his horse without help.

Just then two cowboys rode down the street shooting their guns and yelling *"Yahoo!"* Aaron's horse got scared, very scared, and tried to rise up. She couldn't because she was tied, but she backed away and pulled and pulled until suddenly she was loose! The cowboys saw her break away.

"Hey! Look here!" one of them shouted, seeing a beautiful horse with only a little boy on it.

Aaron hung on for dear life. "Sheriff! Help! Help! Sheriff!" he yelled.

The two men surrounded his horse. They were awful looking. Their faces were a dismal gray color. They wore battered hats, dirty clothes, and their horses were scrawny and had chips in their plastic. One of them grabbed Aaron's horse by the reins.

"Well, well," he laughed, "what have we here? A beauty of a horse and well, well, well, a *deputy!* Why Jeff, will you look at his badge!"

"I'm looking Lefty, I'm looking. Nice and shiny, ain't it? Let's just take the whole lot to Bad Bart. I think he'll like all of it!"

"No!" Aaron screamed. "Sheriff. Help! *Help!* No, don't take me!"

But it was too late. They had his horse and were galloping toward the saloon.

Aaron twisted around in time to see the sheriff and his deputies run out into the street. They started shooting at Bad Bart's men. Aaron ducked to avoid the bullets flying all around him.

This was just what he'd been afraid of. His worst nightmares were all coming true!

All too soon, they arrived at the saloon. Bad Bart's men pulled Aaron's horse to an abrupt stop. Aaron almost fell off.

"Git down," the cowboy called Jeff ordered.

"I can't," Aaron whispered, almost too scared to talk.

"What?" Jeff said.

"I can't," Aaron yelled at the top of his lungs. That got some action. Jeff helped him off and looked at him with some respect.

"Kid's got a good set of lungs. Maybe Bad Bart'll let him join our gang."

"Never!" Aaron yelled.

"Okay, okay. Let's go," said Lefty, and he pushed Aaron into the saloon.

Aaron entered a loud, noisy, dirty room. Lots of rough-looking characters sat on tables playing poker, and drinking. A man ran up and down the piano, playing music. Men and women stood on the bar drinking. A robot made of space Lego pieces helped the bartender.

Lego ladders led up to the bar and the cowboys had to climb them, which wasn't easy with their stiff legs. They did it by swinging their legs over one by one and clamping onto the rungs with their rounded hands. They did the same to get up on the tables. Just as Aaron walked in, a cowboy fell off the bar. It took him forever to reach the floor. But when he did, he bounced on his head, rolled over, jumped up, and started his climb again.

"Lucky he didn't come apart," Jeff muttered. "That there is a loooong fall."

Aaron laughed with relief. Must be nice to be plastic, he thought, so you can't get hurt.

"Somebody tell Bad Bart we've got a present for him," yelled Jeff.

A couple of guys ran through a door in the back.

Soon Bad Bart came out, walking slowly. He was dressed all in black — black hat, black pants, and a black leather jacket. His eyes were bright blue dots, and his face was all white.

Bad Bart looked at Aaron solemnly. He nodded his head and then smiled. "Well young'un," he said in a very deep voice, "you look new to town. I can see you have a deputy badge. What brings you here?"

"None of your business," Aaron replied. Aaron was getting mad. Plenty mad. What right did they have to kidnap him?

"None of my business," Bad Bart repeated. Suddenly the room became deadly quiet.

Everyone looked at Bad Bart's gun. Would the little kid live? No one had ever spoken to Bad Bart that way and lived.

Bad Bart put his hand on his gun. His face looked grim.

"What's the matter," Aaron piped up, "you scared of me?"

Then Bad Bart laughed. He laughed so hard he could hardly stand up. "Am I scared of him? Ha! Ha! Ha! That's a good one."

His face turned serious again. "No, sonny," he said, "I'm not scared. And I'm not mad. You're a brave kid with a lot of spunk. Now what I have here" — and he waved his arms around — "is a special responsibility. Yes, a *very* special responsibility. It's up to me to keep this place as bad as possible, as fun as possible, and as rich as possible. That's what all these people count on me for."

He looked Aaron right in the eye. "Seems to me you might be a valuable addition to our place. You think about it. You'll never escape, you know. So why not join us? You'll be like my very own son. I treat everyone here just like family.

Right, Lefty?" he said, hitting Lefty as hard as he could.

"Right," Lefty agreed, staggering away.

"See," Lefty whispered to Aaron, "he hit me just as if I were one of his own family. Ain't he sweet?"

Aaron was too shocked to reply. Bad Bart wanted *him* to join his gang. He could be a bad guy, shooting and playing with no rules. And he wouldn't get into trouble for being bad.

"Lock him up with the other one while he makes up his mind," Bart commanded.

Jeff grabbed Aaron by the jacket collar and pulled him across the saloon. They went through the back door and were in a hallway with three doors on each side. Jeff unlocked the first door, then shoved Aaron inside.

The door locked behind him. Aaron looked around and saw a bed and a desk.

Otherwise the room was empty.

"Hello," came a voice from above him.

Aaron jumped and looked up. A handsome boy, just his age, hovered in the air, his wings working away. Slowly the boy fluttered to the ground and stood in front of Aaron. He had very blond hair, blue eyes, round pink cheeks, and was dressed all in red velvet, with a gold cap and gold boots.

"Hello," he repeated. "I'm Prince Aryeh. What's your name?"

7

THE GUN FIGHT

"My name is Aaron Samuel," Aaron answered politely, holding out his hand. Prince Aryeh shook it.

"Are you all right?" Aaron asked. "Your wings aren't poisoned? They look fine," he added.

"Oh yes," Prince Aryeh replied, "I'm fine, thank you. I haven't been harmed. What are you doing here?"

"Me? Oh," Aaron said, lowering his voice to a whisper, "I've been sent by your mother to get the sheriff and to help rescue you. Only, when I was waiting on the street for the sheriff, I got captured by Bad Bart's men. Now they want me to join their gang."

"Really?" said the prince. "My mother sent you? But why *you?*"

"Don't you know about the fairy poison?" Aaron asked.

"Oh that's right," Prince Aryeh sighed, "I do know. Bad Bart told me I wouldn't be rescued because of the poison and that I should join his gang. He said I'd be very useful — especially for robberies and that sort of thing, because of course, I can fly in windows."

"Your mother was afraid of that!" Aaron declared. "She worried you might be tempted to join. Are you?"

"We-l-l-l, it *might* be sort of fun, you know," Aryeh said thoughtfully. "I mean, there are so many rules when you're a Prince. You have to behave so perfectly and not make mistakes and not be wild. Sometimes I wish I could be *bad*."

He looked worried. "You won't tell my mother I said that, will you?"

"Oh no," answered Aaron. "Of course not. I know *just* how you feel. People are always saying I'm wild. 'Course my mom says I'm not, I just have more energy than most kids and I'm smart. That's why I act the way I do. But it *would* be fun to be bad, and have no rules and not have to worry about getting into trouble, and not have to go to school."

Prince Aryeh smiled at Aaron. Aaron smiled at Prince Aryeh. They understood each other.

"I still don't know why *you* are here, though," the Prince said.

"I was the only one who answered the fairy call for help. I used to be a big person. I drank something magic and now I'm your size."

"Oh!" exclaimed Prince Aryeh, very much surprised. "I thought you were a fairy like me, but perhaps you'd had an accident and lost your wings. I didn't want to mention it. I thought it might make you feel bad if I did."

"That was very thoughtful of you," replied Aaron. "The potion will wear off in the morning. Then I'll be big again. So I guess I can't really join up with Bad Bart."

He paused. "I didn't *really* want to anyhow," Aaron added. "You know, I'll bet Bad Bart has lots of rules, too. *His* rules. And if we broke them, we'd get into much more trouble than we would at home. And of course, we'd be breaking the law."

"You're right," Prince Aryeh agreed. "Your mother is right, too — you *are* smart. Well," he continued, "do you have any ideas about getting out of here?"

Aaron felt downhearted, and he sat

down on the bed. He shook his head. "No, not any." He looked around the room. "What about the window?"

"It's locked," answered Prince Aryeh.

"Why don't we break it?" Aaron suggested.

"With what?"

"With the chair. They always break windows with chairs in cowboy movies."

"But," Prince Aryeh protested, "a lot of glass will fly around and we would get badly cut."

"Well," answered Aaron, "I'd rather take that chance. Think of what Bad Bart will do to us when he finds out we don't want to join him."

"That's true," said Prince Aryeh. "It'll take two of us."

They picked up the chair and took it over to the window.

Click. The door opened.

"Now, now, now," said Jeff, shaking his

head. "Just what are you little fellows up to?"

"Nothing, nothing," said the two boys, dropping the chair.

"Come with me," ordered Jeff. "Bad Bart wants to hear if you're gonna join up with us or not."

Aaron felt sick when he heard that. He looked at the Prince. The Prince turned a bit green.

"Git going!" ordered Jeff.

Both boys hurried out of the room and down the hallway, into the saloon. When they entered, Bad Bart shouted, "Quiet! Let's hear what these pups have to say."

For a moment neither of them spoke. Finally Aaron thought they might as well get it over with.

"We've decided," he said in his loud voice, so they wouldn't know he was scared, "to — "

Suddenly there was a hollering, a hooting, a screaming, a yahooing. Then guns were fired, and the sheriff and his men burst into the saloon.

"Give up the boys, Bart," the sheriff yelled.

"Never!" exclaimed Bart.

"Never say never!" the sheriff said, and fired at Bad Bart. Bad Bart ducked behind a table leg. Soon all the table legs were being used as shields in a fierce gun fight between the law and the bad guys.

When the first shot was fired, Aaron and the Prince threw themselves to the floor and crawled under the nearest table. After a few minutes, Aaron peeked out from behind a table leg.

"Look, we better get out of here," he whispered to the Prince. "It looks like they just want a good fight. I don't think they care whether *we* get saved, or hurt, or anything."

"I agree," the Prince replied. "Let's

sneak around to the side. Maybe we can slip through the door without anyone seeing us."

Slowly Aaron inched his way around the side of the saloon, Prince Aryeh right behind him. They crawled on their hands and knees. It took about five minutes, but they finally reached the door. No one even noticed them as they slipped away.

"The horses," commanded the Prince. "Grab a horse."

"I can't," Aaron protested, "they're too big."

"It's the only way," Prince Aryeh insisted. "That yellow one looks good. I'll help you, then I'll fly in front, leading her by the reins. If you have to walk, it'll take too long. They'll catch us."

"Well, you fly away," Aaron said. "Don't wait for me."

"Don't be stupid," Prince Aryeh replied. "I wouldn't leave you behind.

You're going to be my best friend, I just know it! Come on now."

And in a flash he had dragged Aaron over to the horse. Pulling him by the arms, the Prince lifted Aaron into the saddle.

"Where do we go?" the Prince said. The sounds of gunshots were still coming from the saloon.

Aaron heard the sheriff yell, "Hand those boys over, Bart, or you'll be sorry." He heard Bad Bart answer, "Never!"

"Behind the sheriff's office," Aaron exclaimed. "That way! There's a helicopter waiting for us."

"Right!" said the Prince. He picked up the yellow horse's reins, and flew off. Aaron had to hang on for dear life. But soon they were at the sheriff's office.

"Behind there," Aaron yelled to the Prince. "Hurry." He turned and looked back.

Bursting out of the saloon and racing down the street came the sheriff and his posse chasing Bad Bart and his men. The boys could hear them hollering.

Prince Aryeh quickly led the horse around the back of the building and through the tall grass until they came to the helicopter. Kim was standing outside it. When she saw them, she ran to Aaron and helped him down from the horse.

"Hi ya kid, how are you? And who's this?"

"I am Prince Aryeh," the Prince replied. "And Aaron has just rescued me from Bad Bart. But," he added, "I suggest we get on our way as they are still after us."

"Good idea," Kim smiled. "Hop in, boys."

Swiftly she helped them into the helicopter, leaped in herself, and revved the engine. Just as the cowboys came into view, the helicopter took off.

Thunk thunk.

"What's that?" Aaron asked.

"I think they're shooting at us," Kim replied.

"Shooting at us!" Aaron said. "Great, just great!"

"Don't worry kid," Kim said, "I'll get us out of here. It's clear sailing — nothing to worry about."

8

ESCAPE!

"I'm going to have to go the long way to get back to the airport," Kim declared. "It would be quicker to travel the way we came but not with those guys shooting at us."

Aaron sagged back into his seat, exhausted but happy. "We did it!" he laughed. "We got away! Your mother is going to be very happy," he said to Prince Aryeh.

"I'm very happy," declared the Prince. They were flying over Legoredo now

and Aaron peered out the window. He watched as they flew over the mining village, the huge Lego statue of Sitting Bull, and the Legoredo railroad. "Wow," he exclaimed, "there's Mount Rushmore with the four presidents. What a great view of them!"

"Guess how many Lego bricks it took to make that copy of Mount Rushmore, with the faces of President Washington, President Jefferson, President Theodore Roosevelt, and President Lincoln?" Kim asked proudly.

"How many?" Aaron asked.

"Guess!"

"A million!"

"Close," Kim chuckled. "In fact it took exactly one-and-a-half million."

"Hey," called Aaron, "there's the roller coaster." The roller coaster was made out of logs. During the day it raced through a course of bushes, waterfalls, and a large

Lego mural showing buffalos being hunted by Indians on horseback.

"I wanna go on that tomorrow," Aaron said.

"What do you mean?" asked Kim. "Small people can't go on those big people rides."

"I can tell you now, Kim," Aaron replied. "I'm not a fairy cousin."

"You aren't?" Kim exclaimed. "Well, kid, what are you then?"

"He's a big person," Prince Aryeh explained, "whom my mother made little so he could come and rescue me."

"Well, now I've heard just about everything," Kim grinned. "How did they manage that?"

"It's a magic drink," Aaron replied. "But it wears off."

"Well, I better get you back to the airport," Kim laughed, "before you get big in my helicopter. That would certainly do some damage! I'm turning now. We'll fly over the Safari Park, then right over Miniland, and on to the palace."

They landed on the roof over the chapel. Prince Aryeh led the two of them down the stairs, into the palace. Martha happened to be coming out of one of the bedrooms when she saw them in the hallway. She screamed with delight.

"Master Aryeh!" she cried, giving him a big hug, "I'm so glad to see you. Are you all right?"

"Yes, Martha," smiled Aryeh, "I am, thanks to my friends here."

"Your mother is in the throne room," Martha said. "She's just had an audience with some important visitors. Follow me, she'll want to see you immediately."

They hurried after Martha and soon found themselves in the throne room. Aaron stopped for a moment just inside the door as Prince Aryeh ran to his mother. Kim waited with him.

Aaron looked around the room. He had never seen anything so magnificent. It was painted in deep brown, red, gold, and black. On one side of the room was King Oberon's throne, on the other, Titania's.

There were flowers everywhere, silver ornaments, antique vases, delicately painted doors, and filigreed windows. In front of Titania's throne were two carved wooden pedestals. On the top of each was a silver horse. Two wide white glass steps led up to the platform on which her throne sat. The throne itself was decorated with a golden peacock ornamented with diamonds, rubies, and sapphires.

Titania sat on the throne, in a gown of fairy silk embroidered with gold, inlaid with pearls, her pearl tiara on her head. Prince Aryeh ran to her and she enfolded him in a loving embrace. She kissed him, and asked him question after question.

When she'd heard his story she beckoned Aaron and Kim up to the throne. Aaron felt a little shy. Everything suddenly seemed so grand. But he forced himself to walk across the room and up the steps to the throne.

The Queen smiled and said, "You were the perfect boy for this mission. We should like to thank you for your bravery, your energy, your intelligence." Aaron blushed. He felt very embarrassed. Then she turned to Kim. "And we should also thank you, Kim. It seems that without you the boys would never have gotten away."

"Well, Your Majesty," answered Kim, "it was a pleasure. And," she added, "I'm sure the sheriff will put Bad Bart in jail where he belongs."

"I'm sure he will," the Queen agreed.

"It's almost morning, Aaron," said the Queen. "We have to get you out of the palace before you grow big."

"Already?" Prince Aryeh objected. "But I want to show Aaron my room and my toys."

"I'm sorry, dear," the Queen replied. "I would love Aaron to stay. I can see you two have become very good friends."

"We have," the Prince beamed.

"You see, Aaron," the Queen smiled, "you don't seem like a wild child to us!"

Aaron smiled, too.

"I wish I could stay," he said, "but I wouldn't want to ruin your home by suddenly growing."

"You're right," sighed Aryeh, and he held out his hand. "Thanks for everything, Aaron. And if you ever come back to Legoland, come to the palace at night. We'll find some of that magic potion for you. Then you and I can play."

The two boys shook hands.

"Well, Aaron," Kim grinned, "see ya, kid. It's been a real adventure."

"Kim," Aaron said, "do you really want to go home?"

"Sure do, kid."

"Well," Aaron said, "I'll see what I can do."

Then Martha came up to them. At a signal from the Queen, she picked up Aaron and flew out of the throne room. "Good-bye, good-bye," Aaron called.

An instant later, Martha was setting him down in the room outside the palace. She kissed him lightly and zoomed off and out of sight.

9

KIDS THESE DAYS!

Aaron sat down and made himself as comfortable as possible on the cold floor. Perhaps he fell asleep because the next thing he knew he was sitting up with a start. He looked around and realized that he had returned to his normal size. Quickly he made his way back to the hotel. He noticed that the sky was getting lighter, the sun about to rise.

Unfortunately the door to his hotel room had locked behind him. He pounded on the door until Rebecca answered it.

His parents were still sound asleep.

She looked at him in disbelief, then said, "Are you gonna be in trouble!"

"Not if you don't tell," he said.

"What were you doing?"

"If I tell you will you keep your mouth shut?"

Rebecca nodded.

Quickly Aaron told her the whole story.

"Boy, do *you* have an imagination," Rebecca said when Aaron had finished.

Aaron just crawled into bed. He was too tired to fight.

"Say," said Rebecca, "what's that in your pocket?"

Out of his pocket Aaron took a tiny blue suede jacket. "Prince Aryeh's jacket," he said. "The one the Queen gave me to wear in Legoland."

Rebecca's jaw dropped.

Aaron smiled and then fell asleep.

A few hours later the family wanted to

go to breakfast but they couldn't wake Aaron.

"Let him sleep," Rebecca said to her parents. "He was up in the night."

"That's strange," said her mother. "I always wake up if he does."

"Not last night," Rebecca said, and then she muttered to herself, "not when there's magic working."

"What?" said her mother.

"Nothing," Rebecca said, "let's come back for him at lunchtime."

Aaron finally woke up a little after two P.M. He had a late lunch, and then they all went to the Legoland Park. Aaron begged to go to the Legoland airport.

When Aaron wanted something badly, he usually got his way and within minutes they were there. He peered over the fence. Yes, there she was. Kim, sitting in her helicopter. He was sure it was her.

Before anyone knew what he was doing

he had jumped the barrier, raced over to the helicopter, taken Kim out, and stuck her in his pocket. Then he was back on the other side. A lot of people had seen him.

"Meet you in Fabuland," he said to Rebecca, "at the Ferris wheel. I gotta get lost in the crowd." And he took off.

He ducked into the crowd. As he looked back, he saw his parents standing there, looking very surprised. Rebecca was explaining to them where he was going.

He heard a lot of indignant adult voices, many speaking Danish, which he didn't understand, but some English, which he did.

"Did you see that kid? What behavior! Wild. Kids these days! Wild. Just wild."

Aaron smiled when he heard and patted his pocket. He wouldn't pay attention anymore when people called him wild — Queen Titania knew it wasn't true. She was proud of him and he felt proud of himself, too.

He was going to mail Kim back to the department store in Minneapolis where she belonged. Wouldn't she be surprised!

And then he ran toward the Ferris wheel to wait for his mother, his father, and his sister.